P9-DFP-849

THE STORY OF THE

UTCRACKER

ALLET

A Random House PICTUREBACK® Book

THE STORY OF THE

NUTCRACKER BALLET

by Deborah Hautzig

illustrated by Diane Goode

Random House New York

Text copyright © 1983 by Random House, Inc. Illustrations copyright © 1986 by Diane Goode. Cover illustration copyright © 2006 by Diane Goode. All rights reserved under International and Pan-American Copyright Conventions. Published in the United States by Random House Children's Books, a division of Random House, Inc., New York, and simultaneously in Canada by Random House of Canada Limited, Toronto.

PICTUREBACK, RANDOM HOUSE and colophon, and PLEASE READ TO ME and colophon are registered trademarks of Random House, Inc.

www.randomhouse.com/kids

Educators and librarians, for a variety of teaching tools, visit us at
www.randomhouse.com/teachers

Library of Congress Cataloging-in-Publication Data
Hautzig, Deborah. The story of the Nutcracker Ballet. SUMMARY: Relates the story of the popular ballet, in which a little girl travels with the Nutcracker Prince to the Land of Sweets. 1. Nutcracker (Ballet)—Juvenile literature. [1. Nutcracker (Ballet). 2. Ballets—Stories, plots, etc.] I. Goode, Diane, ill. II. Title.
GV1790.N8H38 1986 792.8'42 85-30149 ISBN-13: 978-0-394-88178-2 (trade) ISBN-10: 0-394-88178-8 (trade)

Printed in the United States of America 31 30 29 28 27 26 25

t was Christmas Eve and Marie and her brother, Fritz, could hardly wait for the party to start. At last the guests arrived. The drawing room doors were flung open and a brilliance of light and color flooded the hall.

"Oh! It's the most beautiful Christmas tree in the world!" cried the children.

Hundreds of tiny candles twinkled like stars, and all sorts of sparkling ornaments and delicious things to eat hung from the branches. Under the tree were so many presents that the children didn't know what to look at first!

Fritz grabbed a toy horse head mounted on a chestnut stick and galloped wildly around the room.

Marie showed everyone her lovely china doll.

Godpapa Drosselmeir brought out his special gifts. He opened a
tremendous box and out stepped a life-size toy soldier! Drosselmeir wound
it up, and everyone watched in awe as it marched around the room.

Next a toy Harlequin and Columbine stepped out of their giant boxes.
Drosselmeir wound them up and they danced together! The children
clapped their hands in delight.

Then Drosselmeir got out from under the tree his gift for Marie and gave it to her. It was a wooden nutcracker shaped like a little man, with a white cotton beard and a cheerful smile from ear to ear. Though it was a small gift, it was the one Marie loved best of all.

Fritz called the nutcracker an ugly fellow and crammed the largest walnut into the poor nutcracker's mouth. Crack, crack— three teeth fell out.

"Stop it, Fritz! You're hurting him!" cried Marie as she snatched the nutcracker from her brother and cradled him in her arms.

"Keep your broken nutcracker," snorted Fritz. "What's the good of a nutcracker who can't do his job?"

Drosselmeir gave Marie his handkerchief, and she gently tied it around the nutcracker's jaw. Marie vowed to protect the little wooden man forever.

Late that night, after the party was over and everyone was in bed, Marie crept quietly downstairs to the drawing room. The grandfather clock struck midnight. Marie stared at the chiming clock when suddenly Godpapa Drosselmeir appeared sitting at the top!

"Godfather! What a fright you've given me!" cried Marie.

But before she could say another word, the most amazing thing happened.

The tree began to grow bigger and bigger, and the windows and toys and everything in the room grew with it. Now Marie seemed no bigger than a toy the size of the nutcracker!

Just then Marie was surrounded by an army of mice. Led by their king, they drew their swords and marched right up to the toy cupboard to challenge their enemy.

Drums beat, trumpets blared! It was the toys' call to arms. Soldiers, puppets, dolls, and even candy people rushed out. Then out of the cupboard leaped the nutcracker, flourishing his sword and leading the toys to battle.

Rank after rank of mice appeared. Marie watched in horror as the nutcracker's small army was driven back. At last three mice seized the nutcracker's sword.

"Now I have you!" squeaked the king of mice.

Marie could stand it no longer. "Oh, my poor nutcracker!" she cried. Then she threw her left shoe as hard as she could, directly at the king of mice. Instantly the mice disappeared as if by magic.

Marie turned to look at the nutcracker she loved so dearly, and before her eyes the homely nutcracker was transformed into a handsome prince.

"My dearest lady," he said, kneeling before Marie, "you have saved my life. Now let me take you to my kingdom—the Land of Sweets."

Taking her by the hand, he led Marie out the window and into Christmas Wood. The snowflakes tasted like sugar; exquisite little snow fairies danced all around them, beckoning them on.

Marie and the little prince were greeted at his palace by a beautiful lady dressed in gossamer pink and white, who shimmered like a dewdrop.

"She is the Sugar Plum Fairy," said the little prince. He told the Sugar Plum Fairy of his battle with the king of mice and how Marie had saved his life.

The Sugar Plum Fairy gently kissed Marie. Then she clapped her hands, and little angels with golden wings and halos took their places for the fairies' dance honoring the homecoming of the little prince.

"And now," said the nutcracker prince, "to the banquet!" He led
Marie through the dazzling marzipan palace and into a crystal hall,
and together they sat upon a golden throne.

Then Marie and the prince watched in delight as all of his loyal
subjects appeared and one by one performed a dance.

From Russia came the Cossack dancers.

Chinese dancers jumped out of a teapot and did a lively dance.

From France came Mother Ginger and her little puppets, called
Polichinelles. They scampered out from beneath her huge skirt and
did a playful dance.

Then all the flowers of the kingdom assembled for the Waltz of the
Flowers, which was led by the Sugar Plum Fairy.

Marie watched the splendor of the dances as though it were all part of a wonderful dream. "Everything and everyone here is so lovable and full of life," she said. "If only I could stay here forever!"

At last Marie and her nutcracker prince stepped into the royal sleigh drawn by reindeer, and all the loyal subjects stood by to bid them farewell. Marie and the prince waved as the sleigh rose slowly into the glittering sky. Everyone in the Land of Sweets waved back till the sleigh disappeared from sight.

The next thing Marie knew, she was in her own familiar bed.

Marie never told anyone about the beautiful Land of Sweets. But she knew that someday her love for the nutcracker would take her back to that magic kingdom where wonderful things await all who have the eyes to see them.